A Note to Parents

DK READERS is a compelling program for be readers, designed in conjunction with leading literacy experts, including Dr. Linda Gambrell, Professor of Education at Clemson University. Dr. Gambrell has served as President of the National Reading Conference, the College Reading Association, and the International Reading Association.

Beautiful illustrations and superb full-color photographs combine with engaging, easy-to-read stories to offer a fresh approach to each subject in the series. Each DK READER is guaranteed to capture a child's interest while developing his or her reading skills, general knowledge, and love of reading.

The five levels of DK READERS are aimed at different reading abilities, enabling you to choose the books that are exactly right for your child:

Pre-level 1: Learning to read
Level 1: Beginning to read
Level 2: Beginning to read alone
Level 3: Reading alone
Level 4: Proficient readers

The "normal" age at which a child begins to read can be anywhere from three to eight years old. Adult participation through the lower levels is very helpful for providing encouragement, discussing storylines, and sounding out unfamiliar words.

No matter which level you select, you can be sure that you are helping your child learn to read, then read to learn!

LONDON, NEW YORK, MUNICH,
MELBOURNE, AND DELHI

For DK/Brady Games
Publisher David Waybright
Editor-in-chief H. Leigh Davis
Licensing Director Mike Degler
International Translations Brian Saliba
Director of Business Development
Michael Vaccaro
Title Manager Tim Fitzpatrick

Reading Consultant
Linda B. Gambrell, Ph.D.

Produced by
Shoreline Publishing Group LLC
President James Buckley Jr.
Designer Tom Carling, carlingdesign.com

For WWE
Director, Home Entertainment & Books
Dean Miller
Photo Department
Frank Vitucci, Joshua Tottenham, Jamie Nelsen
Copy Editor Kevin Caldwell
Legal Lauren Dienes-Middlen

First American Edition, 2009
09 10 11 10 9 8 7 6 5 4 3 2 1
Published in the United States by DK Publishing
375 Hudson Street, New York, New York 10014

DK books are available at special discounts when purchased in bulk
for sales promotions, premiums, fund-raising, or educational use.
For details, contact: DK Publishing Special Markets,
375 Hudson Street, New York, New York 10014
SpecialSales@dk.com

A catalog record for this book is available
from the Library of Congress.

ISBN: 978-0-7566-5390-3 (Paperback)
ISBN: 978-0-7566-5389-7 (Hardcover)

Printed and bound by Lake Book

The publisher would like to thank the following for their kind
permission to reproduce their photographs:
All photos courtesy WWE Entertainment, Inc.
All other images © Dorling Kindersley
For further information see: www.dkimages.com

Discover more at
www.dk.com

READERS

BEGINNING TO READ ALONE
2

CM Punk™

Written by Brian Shields

DK Publishing

For CM Punk, it was his last chance. His opponent was Extreme Championship Wrestling (ECW) champion John Morrison. It was September, 2007. One month earlier, at *SummerSlam 2007*, CM Punk had battled Morrison for the ECW Championship. That night, he lost. He hoped that this event would end differently.

Morrison stepped onto the ropes and jumped off. But Punk was fast. He stepped away and let Morrison

crash to the mat. Then he lifted
the champ, slammed him back
down, and pinned him.

CM Punk had won his first
championship in WWE.
But it would not be his last.

CM Punk's long road to becoming a top WWE Superstar began in Chicago, Illinois. He was one of four children. At the age of five,

his parents nicknamed him "Punk." The name stuck with him all the way to WWE.

As a child, Punk was a huge WWE fan. His favorites were

"Rowdy" Roddy Piper

Jimmy "Superfly" Snuka

"Rowdy" Roddy Piper and Jimmy "Superfly" Snuka. Watching these two all-time greats battle on television, young Punk knew he wanted to be a WWE Superstar one day. He set his mind to that goal and stuck with it.

As a teenager, he became a fan of punk music. Along with the music, he was drawn to punk's "straightedge" fans. Like them, Punk avoided alcohol, tobacco, and drugs. He had seen too many kids get into trouble because of these things. He promised himself that he would steer clear.

Instead, as a straightedge, he worked hard to make himself and his body better. He stayed focused and clean and never lost sight of his goal: to be a WWE Champion.

CM PUNK

After high school, Punk left home to work on his skills. He joined Ohio Valley Wrestling, a training program run by WWE. There, he gained a lot of fans.

He also caught the eye of WWE officials. Would his hard work pay off with a spot in the big time?

In the summer of 2006, he got the call he had been waiting for. WWE wanted him to join! His hard work and great athletic ability had paid off. CM Punk was born!

CM Punk's Stats and Stuff
- Height: 6'1"
- Weight: 222 lbs.
- Birthplace: Chicago, IL
- Finishing Moves: G.T.S. (Go to Sleep), Anaconda Vise

CM Punk's first match with WWE was part of an ECW event in 2006. He defeated Stevie Richards. He used one of his best finishing moves, the "Anaconda Vise." Punk went on a run of ECW wins. He beat top ECW Superstars like Justin Credible, C.W. Anderson, and Shannon Moore.

Like all rising WWE Superstars, Punk faced many challenges. He challenged Mike Knox and defeated him in their first battle. Then Punk teamed up with

WWE Superstars Triple H, Shawn Michaels, and the Hardy Boys in a match against Knox, Edge, Randy Orton, and Johnny Nitro. Punk's team came out on top!

CM Punk wrapped up his first year as a pro with a victory over *Raw* Superstar Shelton Benjamin. But the best was yet to come.

Punk began 2007 with a setback. His unbeaten streak in singles matches was broken by Hardcore Holly. That same year, Punk picked up his nickname—the "Straightedge Superstar." He also joined his first WWE group, the New Breed, teaming with Elijah Burke, Marcus Cor Von, Matt Striker, and Kevin Thorn.

However, just a few weeks after joining, he quit the group in dramatic fashion. He nailed the leader, Elijah Burke, with his signature "G.T.S." (Go to Sleep) finishing move. Punk was a solo act once again.

In June 2007, a tournament was held to crown a new ECW Champion. Punk defeated his old New Breed teammate, Marcus Cor Von, to advance to the finals.

There, he ran into a red-hot Johnny Nitro, who captured the title. This marked the first of many battles between CM Punk and Johnny Nitro. Later that year, Nitro changed his name to John Morrison. Each time the two men met, the ECW Championship was on the line.

Punk and Morrison clashed at
SummerSlam in August. Morrison
defended his title, beating Punk.
Then came their September
"last chance" battle, won by Punk.
CM Punk's dream came true.
He was ECW Champion at last.

Like all champions, CM Punk had to defend his title against the best WWE Superstars. He took on and defeated Big Daddy V, The Miz, and Mark Henry. Then, in January 2008, Punk lost the ECW Championship to Chavo Guerrero. The loss was tough, but good things were just ahead.

At *WrestleMania XXIV*, in March, CM Punk took part in a

CM Punk's WWE Championship History
- World Heavyweight Championship
- ECW Championship
- World Tag Team Championship (with Kofi Kingston)
- WWE Intercontinental Championship

Money in the Bank Ladder Match.
A ladder is placed in the middle of
the ring. A briefcase is hung above
it. Inside is a contract giving the
Superstar who captures it a shot at
a WWE World Championship
match. The first man to claim
it wins!

Joining CM Punk in this big match were WWE Superstars Chris Jericho, Shelton Benjamin, Mr. Kennedy, Carlito, John Morrison, and Montel Vontavious Porter. Many Superstars made it onto the ladder, only to get thrown off!

Finally, after a long struggle, CM Punk climbed to the top of the ladder. He grabbed the briefcase. This golden chance to fight for a WWE Championship was his. But when would he use it? He wisely chose to wait for the right moment.

CM Punk waited for the right time to cash in his championship contract. Meanwhile, he beat many WWE Superstars. The list included Matt Hardy, Chris Jericho, and Tommy Dreamer. Then, in June 2008, CM Punk decided to make his move. He was going to use his golden contract.

Punk watched from the locker room area as Edge, the World Heavyweight Champion, battled Batista. When Batista knocked down Edge, it was time to move.

CM Punk sprinted into the ring. It took only a few seconds for Punk to pin Edge. CM Punk was the World Heavyweight Champion.

Throughout the rest of 2008, Punk defended his new title against many opponents. He beat the much larger John Bradshaw Layfield, also known as JBL. This made Punk clearly WWE's top Superstar.

At *SummerSlam* that year, JBL challenged Punk again. Once again, Punk beat him to keep his title. At *Unforgiven 2008*, Randy Orton, Cody Rhodes, Ted DiBiase, and Manu ganged up on Punk— before his match even started! As a result, Punk lost his title.

But there were more titles to come. In October 2008 on *Raw*, the "Straightedge Superstar" teamed up with Kofi Kingston. They took on Ted DiBiase & Cody Rhodes in a World Tag Team Championship Match.

DiBiase & Rhodes were two of the thugs who had beaten Punk and cost him his title. He wanted to get some revenge.

That's just what he did. Working together as an unstoppable team, Punk & Kingston beat DiBiase & Rhodes. They captured the World Tag Team titles. CM Punk had now earned three WWE Championship titles.

Early in 2009, Punk added the WWE Intercontinental Championship. He beat William Regal to claim his fourth title. Still, he wanted to be top dog again. That meant regaining the World Heavyweight Championship.

CM Punk's road back to the top began once again in a Money in the Bank Ladder Match at *The 25th Anniversary of WrestleMania.* In the match, he fought against Superstars that included Kane, MVP, Finlay, Christian, Kofi Kingston, Shelton Benjamin, and Mark Henry.

Once again, Punk snatched the briefcase! He was the first WWE Superstar ever to win two Money in the Bank Ladder Matches!

Punk then chalked up wins against Edge, Chris Jericho, and Umaga. Then in June 2009, he cashed in his chance—again! Punk noticed that World Heavyweight Champion Jeff Hardy was exhausted after a match. Punk struck! He pinned Hardy to win back the World Heavyweight Championship. Punk was again on top of WWE.

Not Just in the Ring!
This Superstar has also earned fame outside the ring. CM Punk appeared on the TV shows *Monster Garage* and *Ghost Hunters Live*. No surprise there. He's one guy that could probably scare even a monster or a ghost!

The kid from Chicago has come a long way. Whether talking to kids about staying away from alcohol, drugs, and tobacco, or pummeling opponents in the ring, this WWE Champion is a true Superstar!

CM Punk Facts

- CM Punk's arm is tattooed with good luck charms, but he believes you can make your own luck with hard work.

- One of Punk's oldest tattoos spells out "Straightedge" on his stomach.

- Punk created his in-ring style by mixing fighting skills that he learned from his travels around the world.

- No one knows for sure what the "CM" part of Punk's name means. Punk himself has offered different meanings. Sometimes he even says that it has no meaning.

Index

Anderson, C.W. 12

Batista 22
Benjamin, Shelton
  14, 21, 29
Big Daddy V 18
Brooks, Phillip Jack
  6, 8, 11
Burke, Elijah 15

Cor Von, Marcus
  14, 16
Credible, Justin 12

DiBiase, Ted 25, 26
Dreamer, Tommy
  22

Edge 13
Extreme
  Championship
  Wrestling (ECW)
  4, 12, 16, 18

Guerrero, Chavo 18

Hardcore Holly 14
Hardy Boys 13
Hardy, Jeff 30
Hardy, Matt 22
Henry, Mark 18, 29

JBL 24
Jericho, Chris 22,
  21, 30

Kane 29
Kingston, Kofi 26,
  29
Knox, Mike 12, 13

Layfield, John
  Bradshaw 24

Manu 25
Money in the Bank
  Ladder Match 19,
  29
Moore, Shannon 12
Morrison, John 4,
  16, 17, 21

New Breed 14
Nitro, Johnny 13,
  16

Ohio Valley
  Wrestling 10
Orton, Randy 13, 25

Piper, "Rowdy"
  Roddy 6, 7

Porter, Montel
  Vontavious
  (MVP) 21, 29
Regal, William 28
Rhodes, Cody 25,
  26
Richards, Stevie 12

"straightedge" 8,
  14, 26
Snuka, Jimmy
  "Superfly" 7
SummerSlam 4, 17

Triple H 12

Umaga 30

WrestleMania 18